SIMON AND SCHUSTER

SIMON AND SCHUSTER
First published in Great Britain in 2013 by Simon and Schuster UK Ltd
1st Floor, 222 Gray's Inn Road, London WC1X 8HB
A CBS Company

Based on the television series Mike the Knight

ISBN 978-1-4711-1593-6
Printed and bound in China
10 9 8 7 6 5 4 3 2 1
www.simonandschuster.co.uk

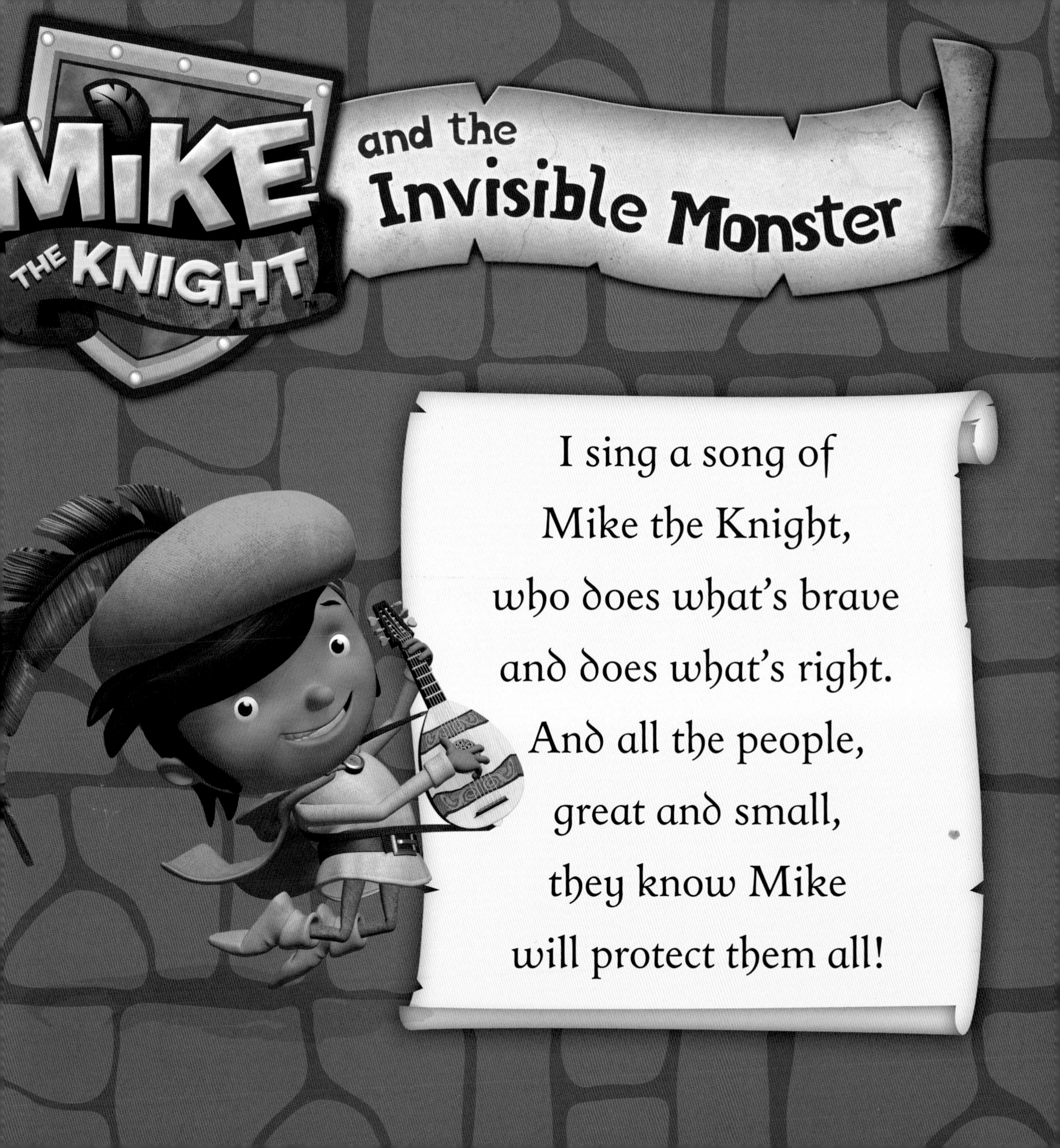
MIKE THE KNIGHT
and the
Invisible Monster
I sing a song of
Mike the Knight,
who does what's brave
and does what's right.
And all the people,
great and small,
they know Mike
will protect them all!

A knight is always on his guard – it's his job to protect the kingdom from danger. Mike and Galahad were patrolling the village. They galloped over the bridge at top speed.

"Whoa! Careful, Mike! You nearly knocked me over!

“Sorry,” called Mike, “but I’ve got things to do.” Protecting the people was important work!

Evie zoomed away on her scooter. Nobody noticed that poor Mr Cuddles had fallen into a deep hole.

"Grrr!"

Suddenly, a roar came from under the bridge.
"Ooh!" trembled Squirt. "It sounds like there's a monster down there! I hope it doesn't attack the village."

The roar came again.

"GGGrrrrrr!"

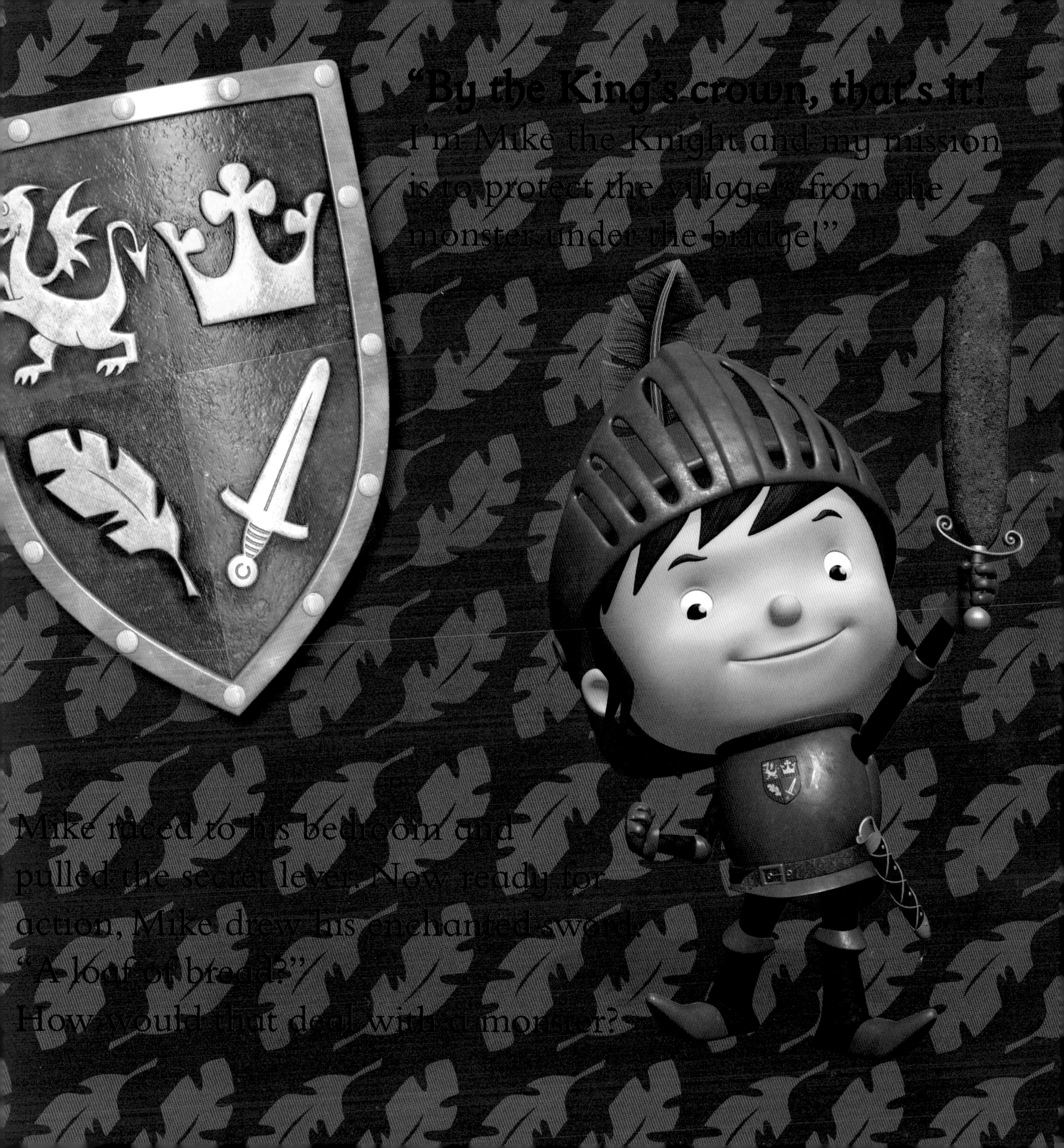

"By the King's crown, that's it! I'm Mike the Knight and my mission is to protect the villagers from the monster under the bridge!"

Mike raced to his bedroom and pulled the secret lever. Now ready for action, Mike drew his enchanted sword. "A loaf of bread?" How would that deal with a monster?

Mike and Galahad rushed into the courtyard. It was time to banish the monster and bravely protect the villagers!

“Do you promise to keep us all safe?” asked Squirt.
“Of course,” replied Mike. “I’m a knight. Onwards!”
“Woo hoo!” cheered Sparkie.

"HUZZAH!" shouted Mike as he raced back to the village to take his place on the bridge.

Before he could start being brave, he needed some villagers to protect. At last, a shepherd appeared.

"Aha!" cried Mike. "Come on, dragons!"

“Stay away from the bridge! There’s a monster under it!” shouted Mike in a stern voice.

The shepherd frowned. He needed to take his sheep into the village.
“What kind of monster is it?” he asked.

"GGrrrrr!"

"It's a Rotten Roaring Monster," announced Mike, "here to scare everyone!"

"We're lucky to have you here to protect us," said the shepherd.

Mike grinned at Galahad. Everyone thought he was really brave!

Before Mike could sort out the monster, he needed the right knightly tools. He asked Sparkie to fetch his lance.

"What's going on here, then?" asked Mr Blacksmith. He wanted to take a pile of wood back to his workshop.

Boom! Boom! Boom!

The monster stomped up and down.

Squirt shivered. "It sounds like it's got really big feet!" "And lots of them," decided Mike. "It must be a Hundred Hooved Monster!"

Sparkie gave Mike his lance so he could deal with the beast under the bridge.

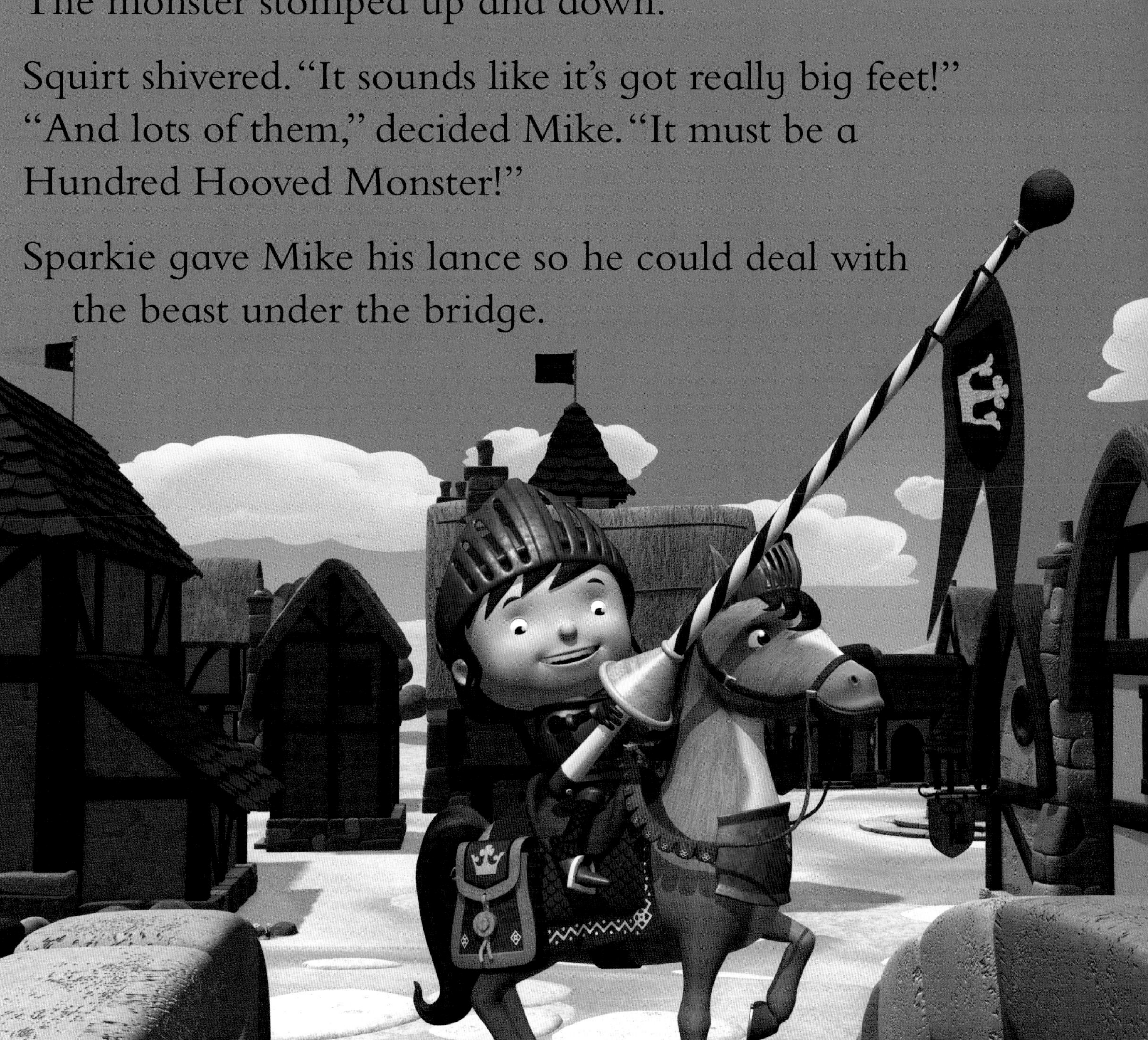

Mike decided not to sort out the monster *just* yet. It was fun being a brave hero! Instead he sent Sparkie to fetch his bow and arrow.

"What's going on?" asked Mrs Piecrust.

"There's a monster," explained Squirt.

Mrs Piecrust looked puzzled. She needed to get to the bakery – she had pies in the oven!

Down in the hole, the monster's tummy started to rumble.

Ru-ru-ru-ru-rurr!

"He sounds hungry," warned Mike. "Like a Huge Hungry Pie-eating Monster!"

When Sparkie got back with his bow and arrow, Mike did some brilliant arrow shooting for the villagers.

"Will you deal with the monster now?" asked Squirt.

Mike gulped. "I'll need... the trebuchet!"

Sparkie rolled the trebuchet up to the bridge.

"There!" said Mrs Piecrust. "Now you can sort that monster out."

"I will," promised the knight-in-training. "I'll just need a..."

Suddenly Evie appeared.

"Help!" she sobbed. "I've lost Mr Cuddles!"

"Evie!" shouted Mike. "Stay away from the bridge!"

"Grrrrr!"

"That sounded like Mr Cuddles," gasped Evie. "I've got to save him!"

"Wait," said Mike. "If anyone should save Mr Cuddles, it's me."

Even though he'd had lots of fun pretending to be brave, he hadn't actually done anything brave yet.

"It's time to be a knight and do it right!" he declared. **"Mike the Knight to the rescue!"**

Mike drew his enchanted sword. Then he peered down the hole. There, right at the bottom, was Mr Cuddles!

"Watch out for the monster!" called Mr Blacksmith.

"It's no good," sighed Mike. "I can't reach Mr Cuddles – the hole's too deep."

"I wasn't so brave after all," said Mike.

Evie disagreed. Mike had been brave even when he thought there was a monster under the bridge.

Everyone cheered. **"HUZZAH!"**

MiKE
THE KNIGHT

MiKE THE KNIGHT
How to Be a Knight
A POP-UP BOOK!

MiKE THE KNIGHT
Mike's Missions
As seen on TV
Press the button
Be a knight, do it right!

MiKE THE KNIGHT
Meet Mike!
As seen on TV

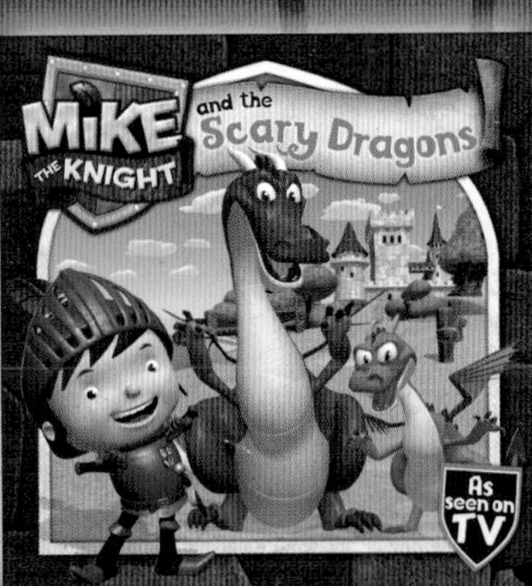
MiKE THE KNIGHT
and the Scary Dragons
As seen on TV

MiKE THE KNIGHT
and the Mighty Shield
As seen on TV

MiKE THE KNIGHT
and the Fluttering Favour
As seen on TV

MiKE THE KNIGHT
and Trollee in Trouble
As seen on TV

MiKE THE KNIGHT
and the Real Sword
As seen on TV

MiKE THE KNIGHT
The King's Crown
Sticker Book
As seen on TV
With Stickers Galore!

More magical
Mike the Knight books